The Gumbo Gators

Written and Illustrated by

Paul Schexnayder

PELICAN PUBLISHING

New Orleans

ISBN: 9781455627011
Ebook ISBN: 9781455627028

Printed in Korea
Published by Pelican Publishing
New Orleans, LA
www.pelicanpub.com

To all the great cooks and chefs of Louisiana,
thank you for your delicious gumbos.
To Fran and Van, thank you for showing up in
my mind. I hope we can go on many more
adventures together.

Down in the swamps of Louisiana lived a happy Cajun couple, Fran and Van Harahan.

Years ago, they moved from the oilfields to the islands. They had homes at Avery Island, Pecan Island, and Marsh Island.

Fran made a shopping list and Van checked it twice.

Everyone knows that alligators hunt for food but Fran and Van now shop by boat.

"Where we going, Van?"

"We're going to be makin' groceries all over the state. Let's head north first."

"Lafayette?"

"Mais* no, Fran. Way north!

"Alexandria?"

"No, chère.** Shreveport!"

"Cawww!"

*mais: French for "but"
**chère: French for "dear" (feminine)

On their way they made a pass through the Bayou Teche area for one bottle of Cajun hot sauce, two loaves of French bread, and three pounds of shrimp.

Up the Vermilion River around Acadiana they got four links of smoked sausage, shook their tails to some Zydeco music, and snacked on some boudin.

"Van, head west now for five bags of rice, then under that tall bridge for six pounds of flour and seven bottles of oil."

From there, Fran and Van motored to the Crossroads in Central Louisiana for eight pods of okra and nine Mardi Gras chickens.

"You coo-yon.* Stop here for that eleven-dollar gumbo pot!"

*coo-yon: Cajun French for foolish one

The boat rocked and rolled northwest on the Red River, stopping for twelve cups of potato salad and then . . .

straight east through Sportsman's Paradise. They saw thirteen deer, fourteen ducks and fifteen geese.

Fran and Van were halfway through makin' groceries when they splashed down on the mighty Missasip'.

Twisting and turning down Old Man River . . .

they stopped for
sixteen onions right
before they entered
the River Parishes.

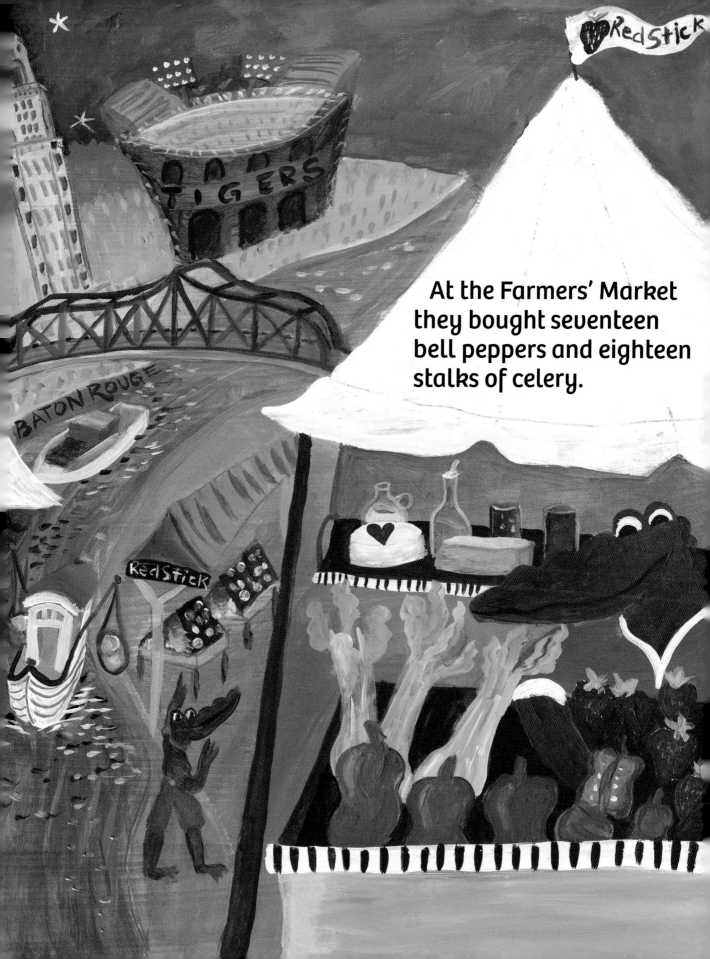

At the Farmers' Market they bought seventeen bell peppers and eighteen stalks of celery.

Van had to pay close attention to all the paddlewheel boats and barges in this part of the river.

N.O. Towing

Fran stood up and yelled, "Throw me something, mister!" The man at the dock gave her the biggest king cake ever. She winked at Van and said, "Ma dessert, sugar!"

It was almost sunset when they made it to the southeast coast near Highway 1 and caught nineteen blue point crabs . . .

Thibodaux

Houma

LA 1

cut off

Galliano

and hauled in a twenty-
pound sack of salty oysters.

Golden
Meadow

Grand
Isle

A soft breeze blew over them as their little boat followed the Old Spanish Trail. Van stopped for a cypress spoon for da roux and Fran picked some low-hanging moss for the fire.

As the boat sputtered into their dock, Van let out a loud yawn.

"Mais, I'm tired," said Van.

"Me too, honey," said Fran.

"I'll let you cook that gumbo tomorrow morning," Van said with a slight grin.

Shaking her head, Fran said, "Van, you always know how to stir dat pot."